# Wake Up, Island

## Mary Casanova

Woodcuts by
Nick Wroblewski

University of Minnesota Press
Minneapolis · London

While you
sleep,

the day is
dawning.

Sunlit fingers
touch the shores.

Water tickles
island's edges.

Wake up, wake up—

night is done.

Pine trees s t r e t c h
their limbs and branches.
Lichen warms on ancient rock.

Doe and fawn rise from their grass bed,

dip their heads to glassy lake.

Pearls of dew
on strings of silver . . .
Spider's work on
fine display.
From a single
thread
she dangles

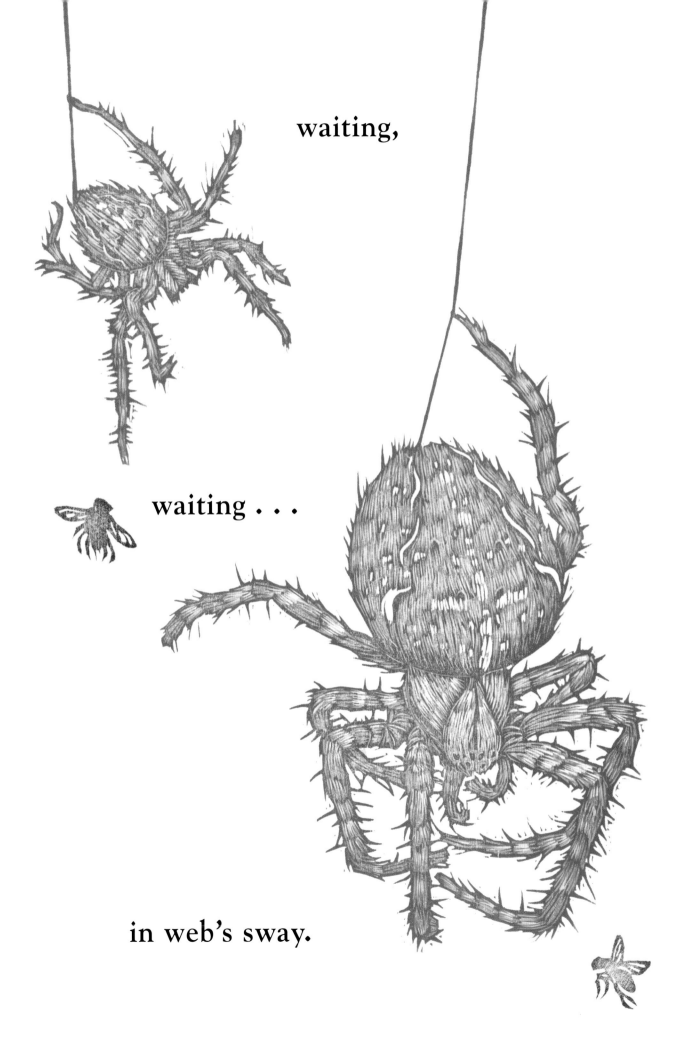

waiting,

waiting . . .

in web's sway.

Moose and calf
plunge into shallows,

graze on underwater

shoots.

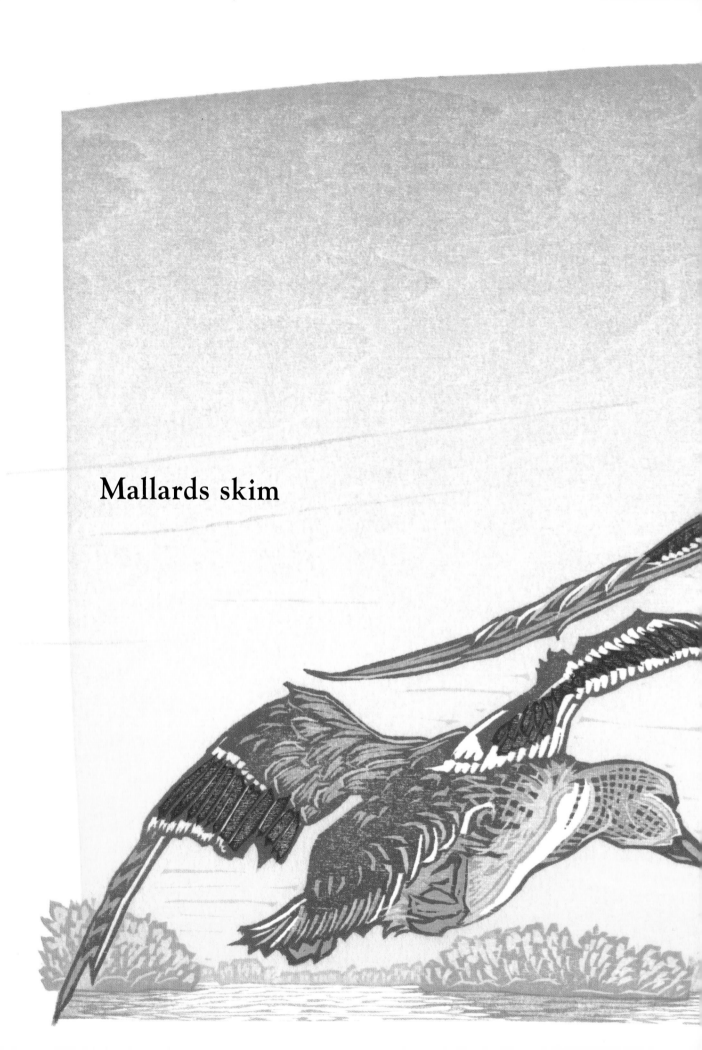

Mallards skim

on wings wuff-wuffing,

rising

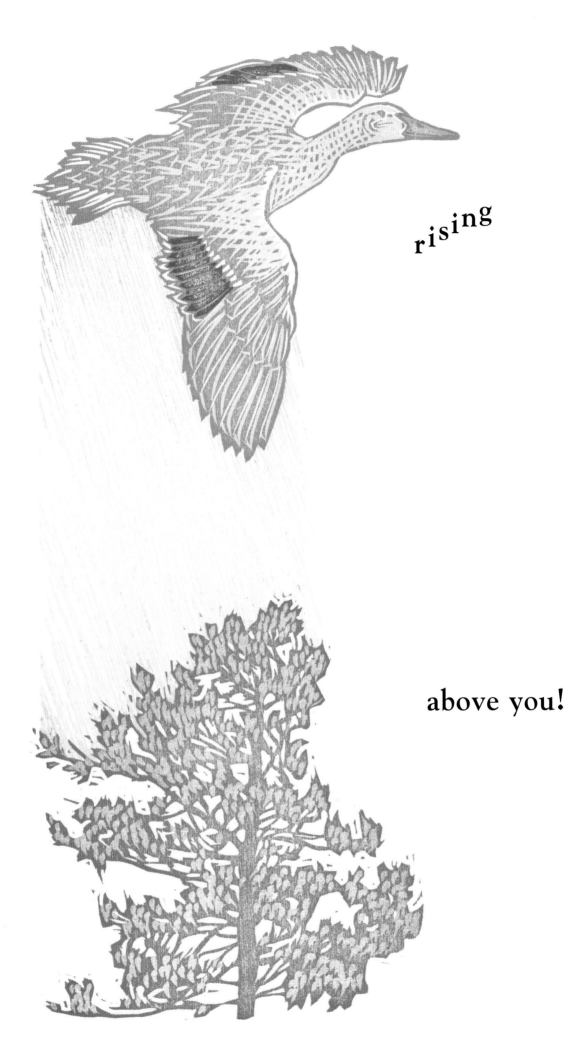

rising

above you!

Ravens perch
and gargle greetings.
Chickadees call
dee,

dee,

dee!

Heron swoops,

a two-stilt statue

watching,

watching . . .

minnows flee!

Red squirrel

chatters, chitter-cheeeeee!—

gathers pine cones

one,

two,

three—

munching,

crunching,

seed

by

seed.

Black bear scratches,

shimmies downward,

roots in logs for ants and grubs.

Bees take flight and

yarrow,

buzz to flowers—

goldenrod.

daisies,

Sunshine
pokes          inside your window,

makes your sleepy eyes
blink wide!

Maple syrup, berry pancakes!

Quickly, quickly—

run outside!

You skip down
as loon
sings
greetings,

leave your footprints—

one by one.

Dipping,

diving,

splashing,

laughing . . .

Wake up, island!

Day's begun.

Mary Casanova has written more than thirty books for young readers, ranging from picture books to novels. Her books have received many awards, including two Minnesota Book Awards. She lives with her husband and three dogs in Ranier, Minnesota, near the Canadian border.

Nick Wroblewski is an artist and printmaker specializing in handmade woodcut blockprints. He prints from his home studio in the Driftless region of Wisconsin. A native of Minnesota, he enjoyed reflecting on a landscape very close to his heart while illustrating this book.

*To the Oberholtzer Foundation, with gratitude*
*—M. C.*

*For Whitman and, of course, the one from which he came*
*—N. W.*

The University of Minnesota Press gratefully acknowledges the generous assistance provided for the publication of this book by the Margaret W. Harmon Fund.

Published by the University of Minnesota Press
111 Third Avenue South, Suite 290
Minneapolis, MN 55401-2520
http://www.upress.umn.edu

Library of Congress Cataloging-in-Publication Data
Title: Wake Up, Island / Mary Casanova ; woodcuts by Nick Wroblewski.
Description: Minneapolis, MN : University of Minnesota Press, [2016].
Identifiers: LCCN 2015026764 | ISBN 978-0-8166-8935-4 (hc) | ISBN 978-0-8166-8936-1 (pb)
Subjects: | CYAC: Islands—Fiction. | Morning—Fiction. | Nature—Fiction.
Classification: LCC PZ7.C266 Wak 2016 | DDC [E]—dc23

Printed in China on acid-free paper

The University of Minnesota is an equal-opportunity educator and employer.

22 21 20 19 18 17 16          10 9 8 7 6 5 4 3 2 1